Day of the Tornadoes

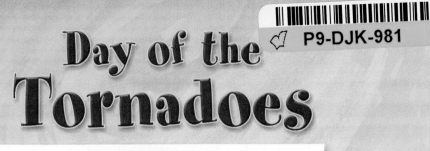

by Gary Miller

Strategy Focus

Tornadoes are powerful and sometimes deadly. As you read, think about **questions** you have about these dangerous storms.

HOUGHTON MIFFLIN

BOSTON

Key Vocabulary

collide to bump or slam into something

funnel cloud a tornado cloud that is wide on top and narrow at the bottom

jagged having a sharp, uneven edge

lightning a flash of light in a stormy sky

prairies flat, open grasslands

rotate to swirl in a circular motion

severe serious or extreme

sizzling crackling with heat

tornadoes windy storms with funnel clouds

Word Teaser

I can travel ten miles in less than a second, and I'm hotter than the surface of the sun. What am I?

Few things in nature are more powerful than tornadoes. Their winds rage. They can strike without warning. They can destroy everything in their path.

Tornadoes often develop from big thunderstorms. Clouds grow dark. Thunder booms. Jagged, sharp bolts of lightning pierce the sky. The air seems to be sizzling or crackling with electricity.

Sometimes the clouds in a thunderstorm start to rotate. They turn faster and faster, forming a funnel cloud that looks like a spinning toy.

Some funnel clouds disappear and do no harm. But others turn into raging tornadoes. A tornado's funnel cloud can spin at more than 300 miles an hour. When it touches down on the ground, it can cause terrible damage.

One tornado is bad enough. But imagine more than 100 tornadoes hitting different places in a single day! That's what happened during the Super Tornado Outbreak of 1974.

The Outbreak began on April 3. It lasted just 24 hours. But in that time, 148 tornadoes swept across 13 states. The tornadoes killed more than 300 people. They injured more than 5,000 others. They destroyed homes, schools, and businesses.

The tornadoes happened in an area known as Tornado Alley. Tornado Alley is in the central United States. The land there is mostly flat. It contains many prairies, or grasslands.

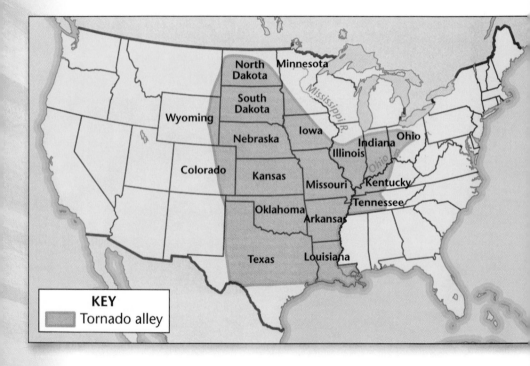

KEY
Tornado alley

Tornado Alley often has storms in the spring and summer. Streams of cool, dry air collide with, or bump into, warm, wet air. When the two kinds of air hit each other, they often cause severe weather. Sometimes that means tornadoes.

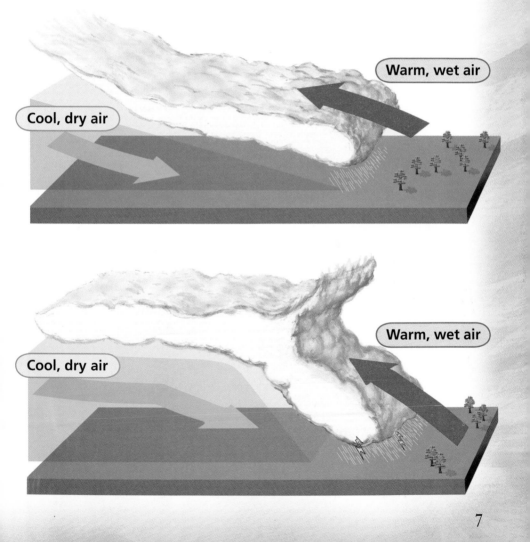

Warm, wet air

Cool, dry air

Warm, wet air

Cool, dry air

The 1974 Super Tornado Outbreak started out as a huge line of thunderstorms. The first tornado broke out in Morris, Illinois.

Soon, tornadoes were forming all along the line of the storm. The storm's path was more than 2,500 miles long. It ran from Mississippi all the way to Virginia.

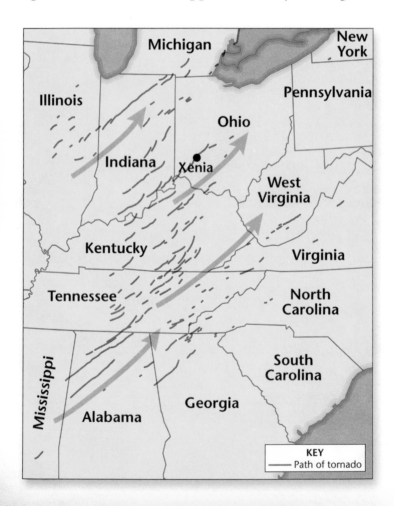

Not all the tornadoes in the Outbreak were the same. The shortest tornado probably lasted only minutes. The longest one lasted two hours. Some were stronger than others, too. Six tornadoes reached an F5 class. That's the strongest kind of tornado. It has winds of more than 261 miles an hour.

Tornado Scale

Scale	Wind Speed
F0	40–73 miles per hour
F1	73–112 miles per hour
F2	113–157 miles per hour
F3	158–206 miles per hour
F4	207–260 miles per hour
F5	261–318 miles per hour

One of the F5 tornadoes touched down in Xenia (ZEE-nee-uh), Ohio. In about a minute, it destroyed much of the city.

The tornado ripped trees from the ground. It tore down buildings and homes. It tossed cars and trucks into the air. It wiped out more than 1,300 buildings, including several schools.

Luckily, the tornado hit after school had ended for the day. Most children weren't in the buildings. But not everyone escaped safely. More than 30 people were killed in Xenia.

Some of the terrible damage in Xenia, Ohio.

Many other tornadoes caused serious damage. Most people had little warning. Back in 1974, scientists had no tools to predict tornadoes. So, no one knew a tornado was coming until someone saw it.

In Xenia, people found out about the tornado just 15 minutes before it hit. The warning probably saved some lives.

Today, scientists have many tools to warn us about severe weather. The tools show where thunderstorms are and whether tornadoes might form.

But it's still hard to know when a tornado will hit. These storms are very hard to predict.

Today, people use computers and other equipment to help predict bad weather.

Will another super tornado outbreak happen? No one knows. But weather experts will be keeping a close watch on the sky.

Staying Safe During a Tornado

✓ If you are outside, try to stay in a ditch or another low place.
✓ If you are inside, try to stay in a basement or a storm cellar.
✓ Stay away from windows and doors that lead outside.

Putting Words to Work

1. What kind of **severe** damage can a tornado cause?

2. Complete the following sentence:
   When two objects **collide**, they _____.

3. Describe how a **tornado** forms, using at least two of the
   following words: **collide, funnel cloud, lightning,
   rotate**. Be sure to put the steps in the right order.

4. Would you like to see a **tornado** in action? Why or why not?

5. **PARTNER ACTIVITY:**   Think of a word you learned in
   the text. Explain its meaning to your partner and give
   an example.

Answer to Word Teaser
lightning